Toot & Puddle

by
Holly Hobbie

Little, Brown and Company
Boston New York London

First Travel Edition

Library of Congress Cataloging-in-Publication Data

Hobbie, Holly.
    Toot and Puddle / by Holly Hobbie. — 1st ed.
        p. cm.
        Summary: Toot and Puddle are best friends with very different inter-
ests, so when Toot spends the year traveling around the world, Puddle
enjoys receiving his postcards.
    ISBN 0-316-36552-1 (hc) / ISBN 0-316-14569-9 (travel)
    [1. Pigs — Fiction. 2. Travel — Fiction 3. Friendship— Fiction.
4. Postcard — Fiction.]   1. Title
PZ7.H6515Ad   1997
[E] — dc20   96-28649

                            HC: 10 9 8 7
                            TR: 10 9 8 7 6 5 4 3 2 1

                                SC

                        Printed in Hong Kong

        The paintings for this book were done in watercolor.
    The text was set in Optima, and the display type is Windsor Light.

Toot and Puddle lived together in Woodcock Pocket.

It was such a perfect place to be that Puddle never wanted to go anywhere else.

Toot, on the other hand, loved to take trips. He had been to Cape Cod, the Grand Canyon, and the redwood forests.

One day in January, Toot decided to set off on his biggest trip ever. He decided to see the world. "Do you want to come along?" he asked Puddle. "We could start with someplace warm and wild."

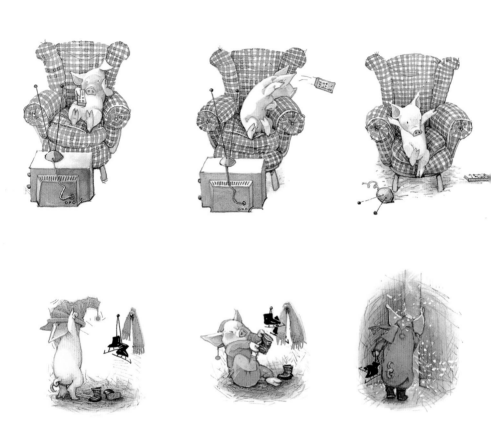

Puddle preferred to stay home.

I love snow, he thought.

Dear Puddle,
I've made some
new friends in
Africa! Is winter
getting boring?

Toot

To: Puddle
Woodcock Pocket
U.S.A.

FEBRUARY AM 1997 KENYA AFRICA

PAR AVION

Meanwhile . . . presenting Puddle at Pocket Pond!

MARCH ON THE NILE

Dear Puddle,
  EGYPT is awesome.
The Pyramids are
the greatest. Wish
You could MEET me
at the Oasis.
    Your Friend,
      TOOT

To: Puddle
  Woodcock Pocket
     U.S.A.

PAR AVION

March meant maple syrup. Puddle wished Toot were there to taste the pancakes.

Dear Puddle,
    Can you believe I'm
in the Solomon Islands?
They're in the Pacific
Ocean. I spend all day
underwater. I love
being in a school —
of fish. Has Spring
come yet?
        Your pal,
        Toot.

Puddle
Woodcock Pocket
U.S.A.

APRIL
AM
SOLOMON ISLANDS

SOLOMON
ISLANDS

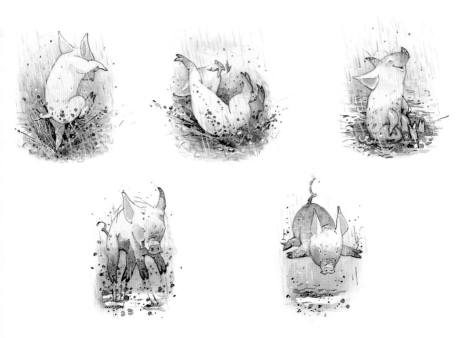

Yes, spring had arrived. Puddle was having mud season. Yay!

Hi, Puds,
Am I in INDIA, or
is this a dream?
It's your birthday—
May 3! Hope your
party is the best.

Friends Forever,
Toot

Puddle
Woodcock Pocket
U.S.A.

PAR AVION

MAY
AM
BOMBAY INDIA 1997

INDIA

Back at Woodcock Pocket . . .
"For he's a jolly good fellow,
for he's a jolly good fellow,
for he's a jolly good fellow,
that nobody can deny!"

Dear Puddle,
    Help! Mountain
climbing is scarier
Than jumping out of
a plane. Remember
when I talked you into   To:
going parachuting?   PUDDLE
Your friend in the Alps,   WOODCOCK POCKET
        Toot   U.S.A.

Puddle remembered.

In July . . . presenting Puddle at Pocket Pond! Every time he jumped in, he cheered, *"Olé!"*

Dear Puddle,
    August is cold in
Antarctica, but I've
made more friends
here than anywhere
yet. Are you going
to the beach this
year? I miss you.
Do you miss me?
    Friends Forever,
        Toot

To: Puddle
Woodcock Pocket
U.S.A.

SOUTH GEORGIA AUGUST PM
SOUTH POLE

Yes, Puddle missed his friend.

Dear Pudsy,
Bonjour from Paris!
Art is everywhere!
Love is in the air!
Au revoir,

Toot

To:
Puddle
Woodcock Pocket
U.S.A.

I love art, thought Puddle.

Dearest Pudsio,
Italy is heaven -
it's one big treat!
Your Friend,
Tootsio

ITALY

OCTOBER
FLORENCE ITALY
AM

To:
Puddle
Woodcock Pocket
U.S.A.

VIA AEREA

Meanwhile, it was Halloween in Woodcock Pocket.

Puddle decided to be horrifying.

One morning in November, Toot woke up and thought, *It's time to go home.*

Yay, Toot's coming!

December called for celebration.
"Here's to all your adventures around the world," said Puddle.
"Here's to all your adventures right at home," said Toot.

"And here's to being together again," Toot and Puddle
said at the same time.

Toot was happy to be back in his own bed, and
Puddle was happy, too.

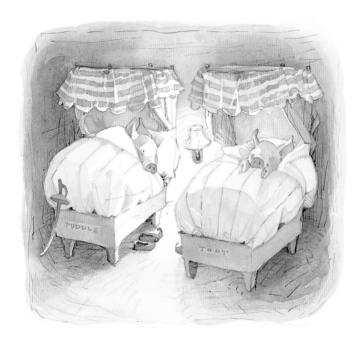

"I wonder if it will snow all night," Puddle said.
"I hope so," said Toot.
"Then we'll go sliding," said Puddle.
"And skiing," said Toot.
"Good night, Toot."
"Good night, Puddle."